Hattie Hippo

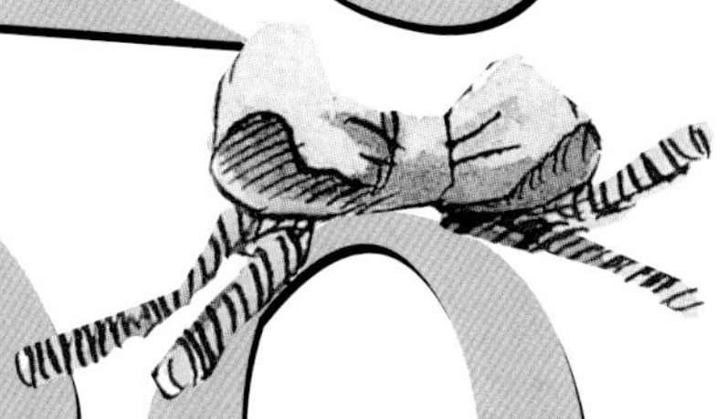

By
Christine Loomis

Pictures by
Robert Neubecker

ORCHARD BOOKS / NEW YORK
AN IMPRINT OF SCHOLASTIC INC.

LIBRARY OF CONGRESS CATALOGING-IN-PUBLICATION DATA IS AVAILABLE.

ISBN 0-439-54340-1

10 9 8 7 6 5 4 3 2 1   06 07 08 09 10

Printed in Singapore   46

Reinforced Binding for Library Use

First edition, August 2006

The art was created using watercolor and ink.

The text and display type were set in 28-point P22 DaddyO Hip.

Book design by Marijka Kostiw

For Kira Rose, with love —C. L.

For Ruth, Iz, and Jo —R. N.

THE BALLET

Hattie Hippo
pirouettes
on teensy, tiny toes.

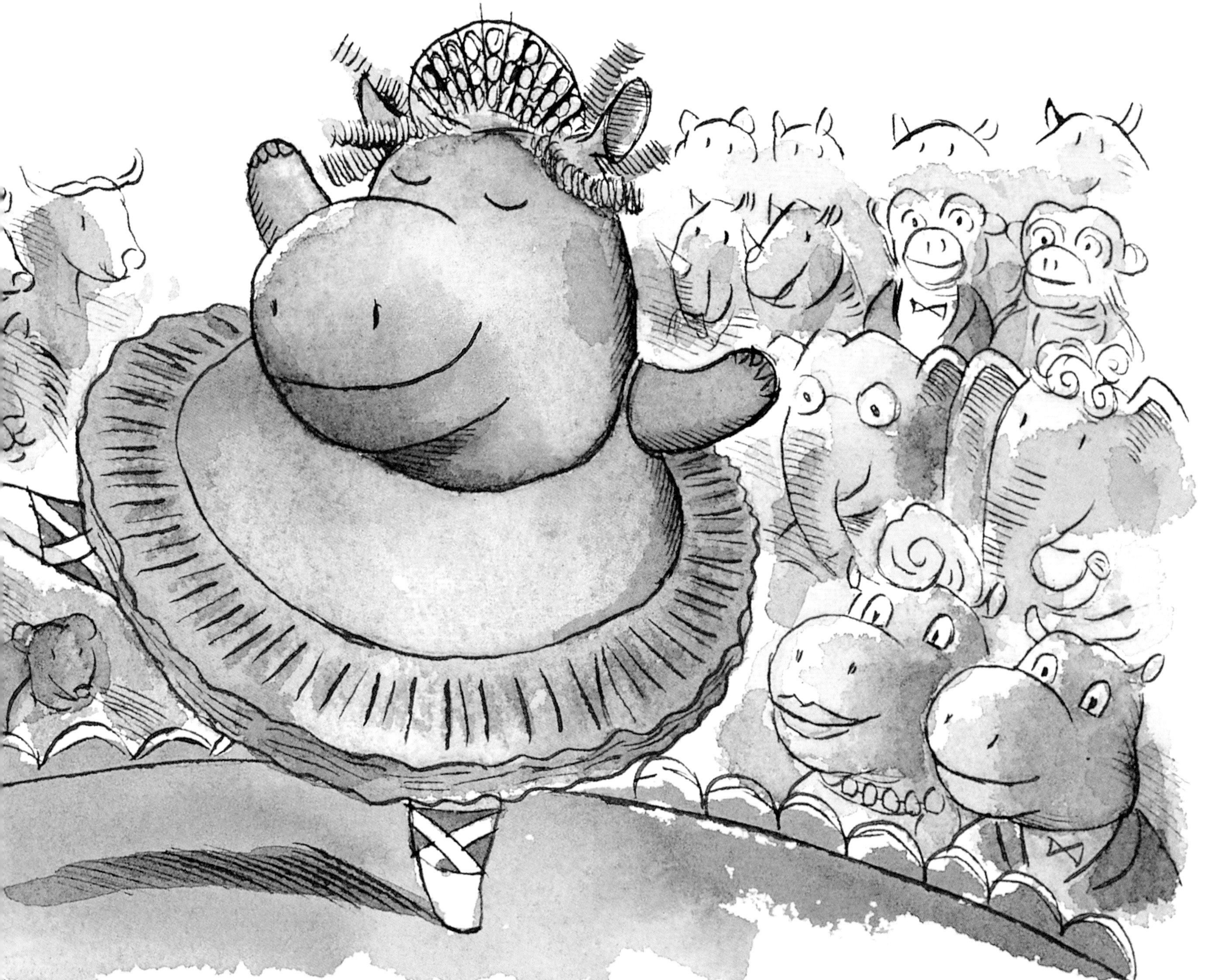

In dazzling,
pearly, perfect teeth
she holds a
pale pink rose.

She whirls,

she twirls . . .

she leaps up high.
Two rhinos,
waiting, smile.

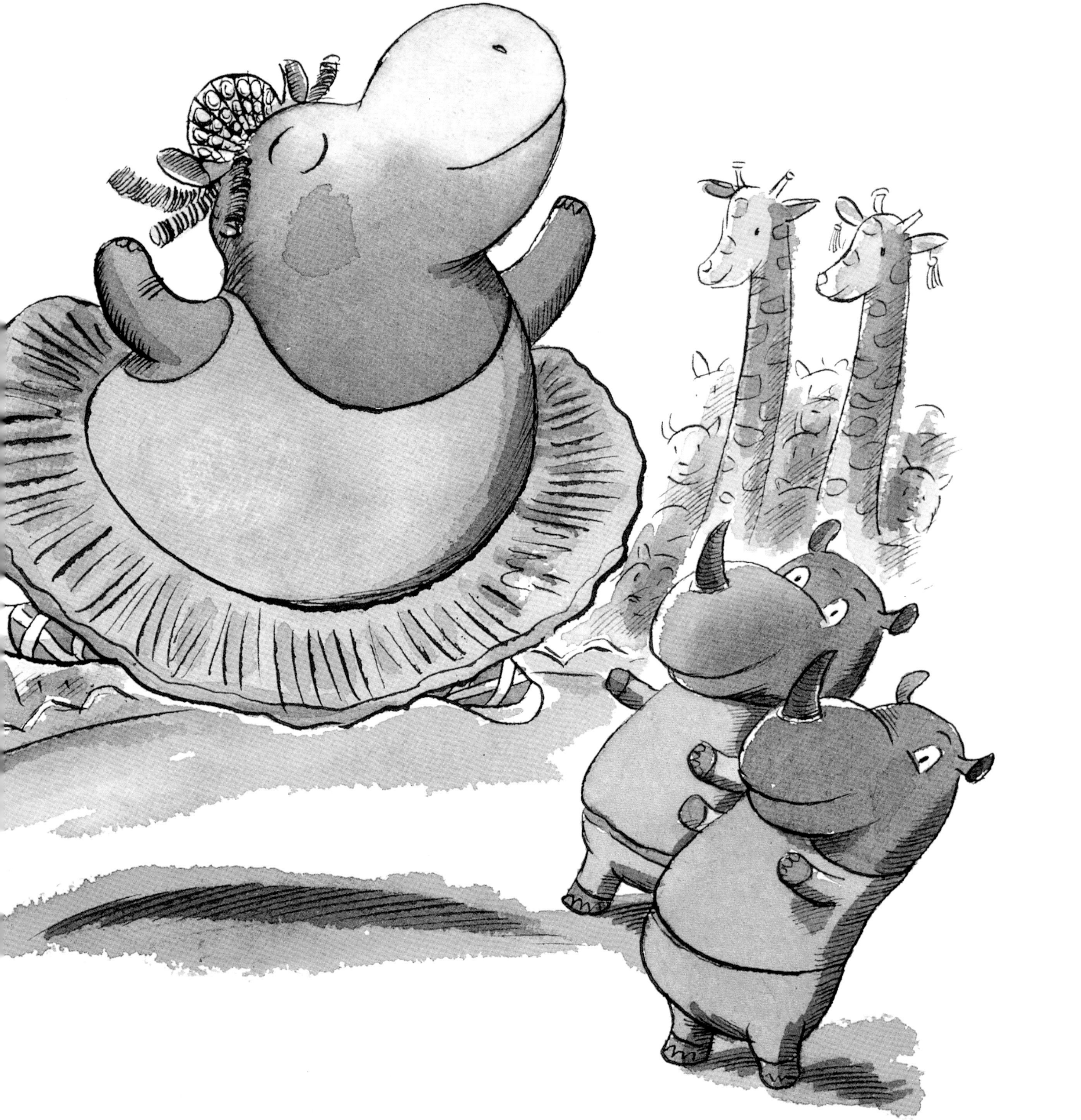

Oops!

Teeny prima
ballerina
misses by a mile!

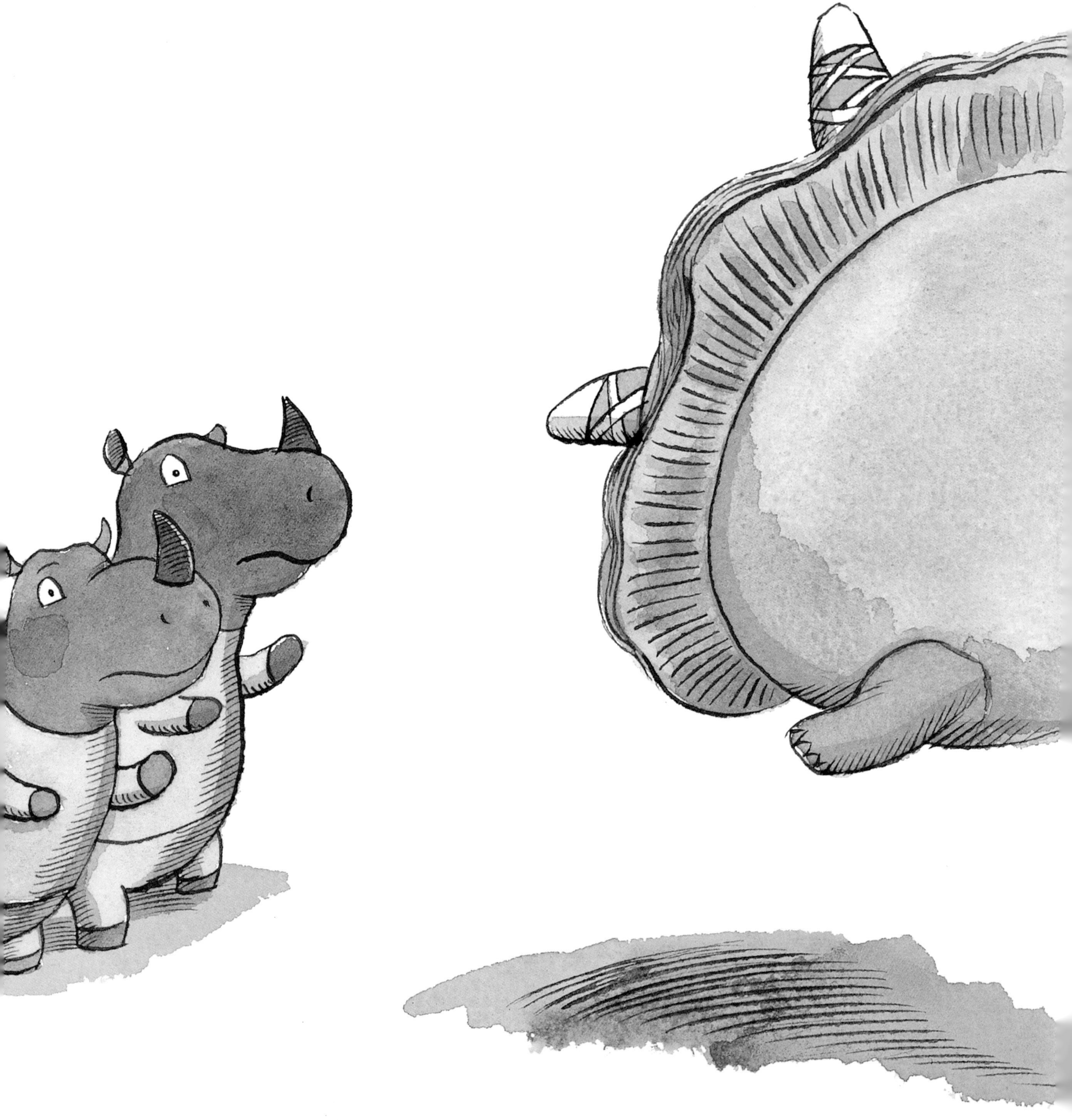

THE TEA PARTY

Hattie Hippo
makes a pot
of cherry berry tea.

She bakes a cake
and lays a cloth

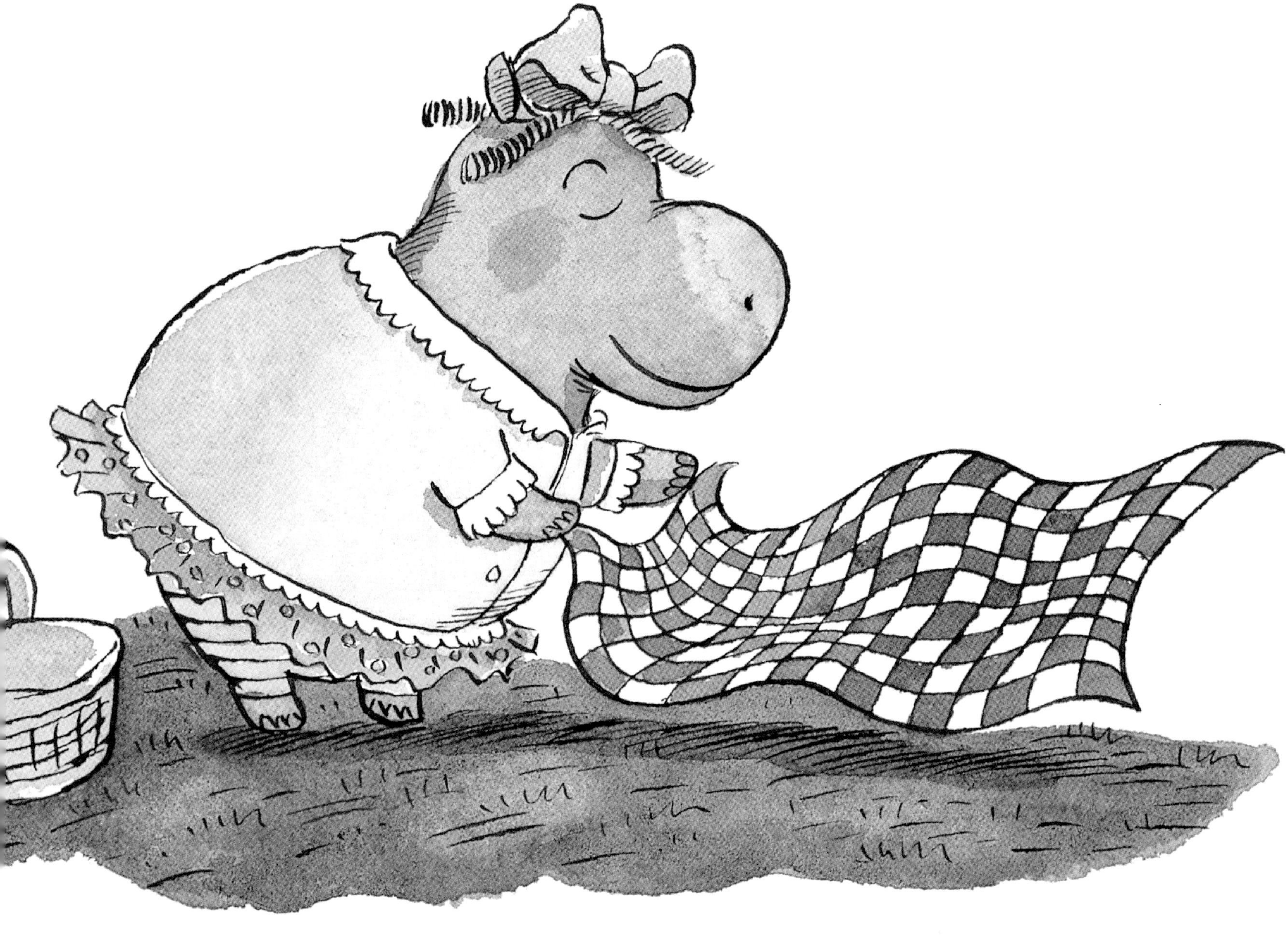

underneath a tree.

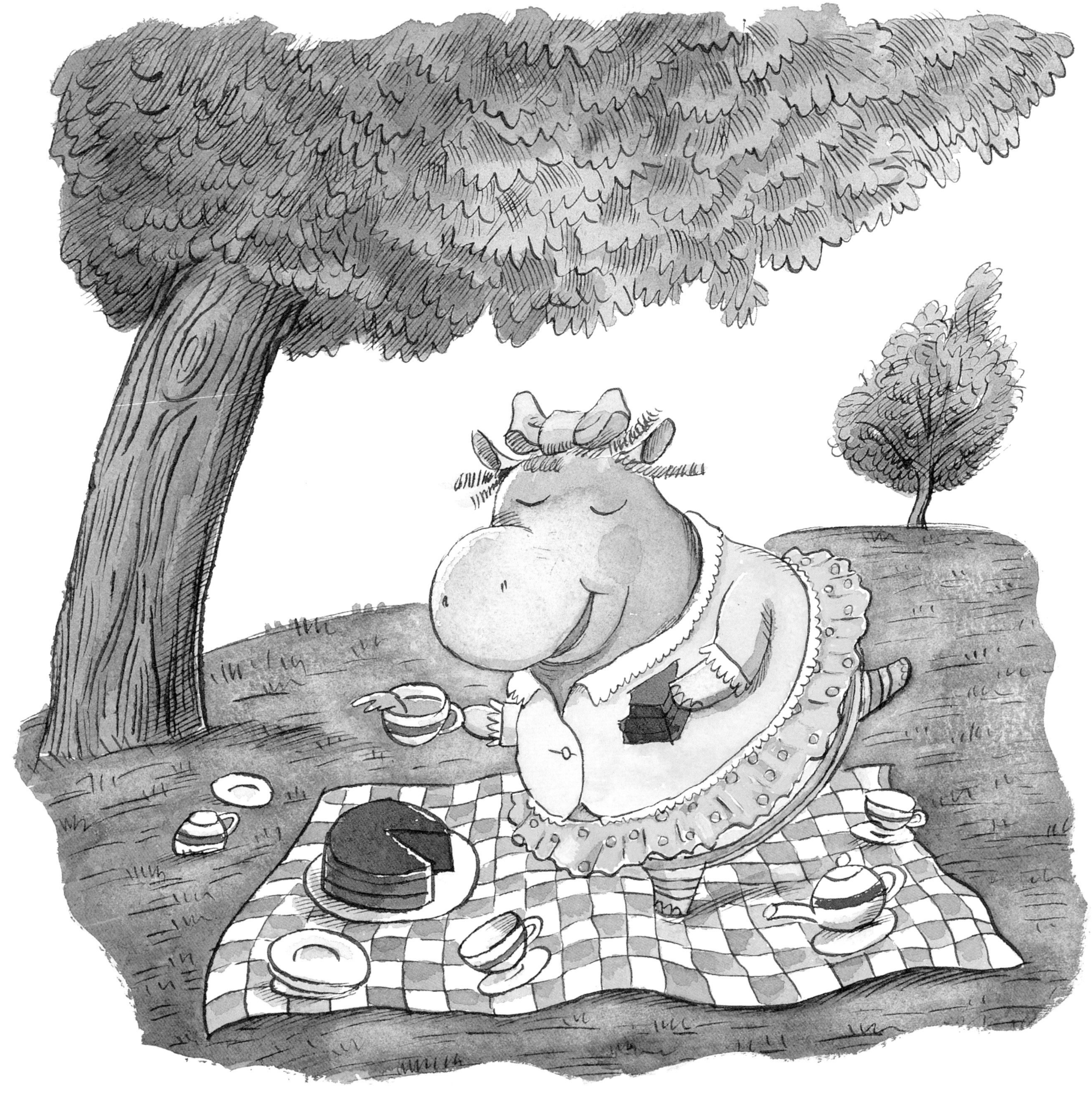

Her guests arrive
and wait and wait
without a crumb or cup.

Oops!
Hattie Hippo ate the cake
and drank
the tea all up!

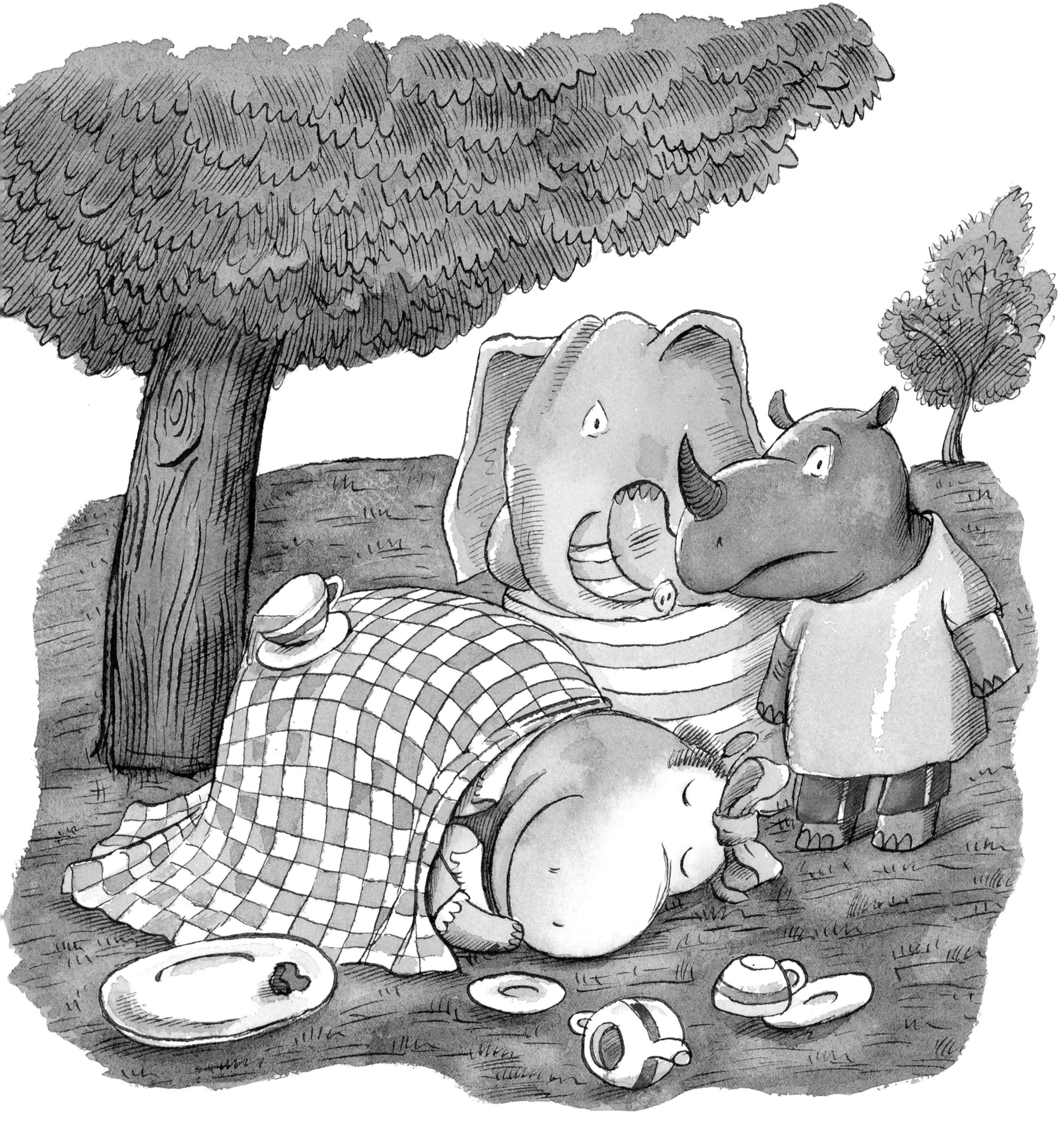

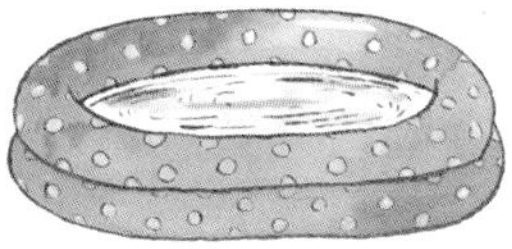

The Swimming Pool

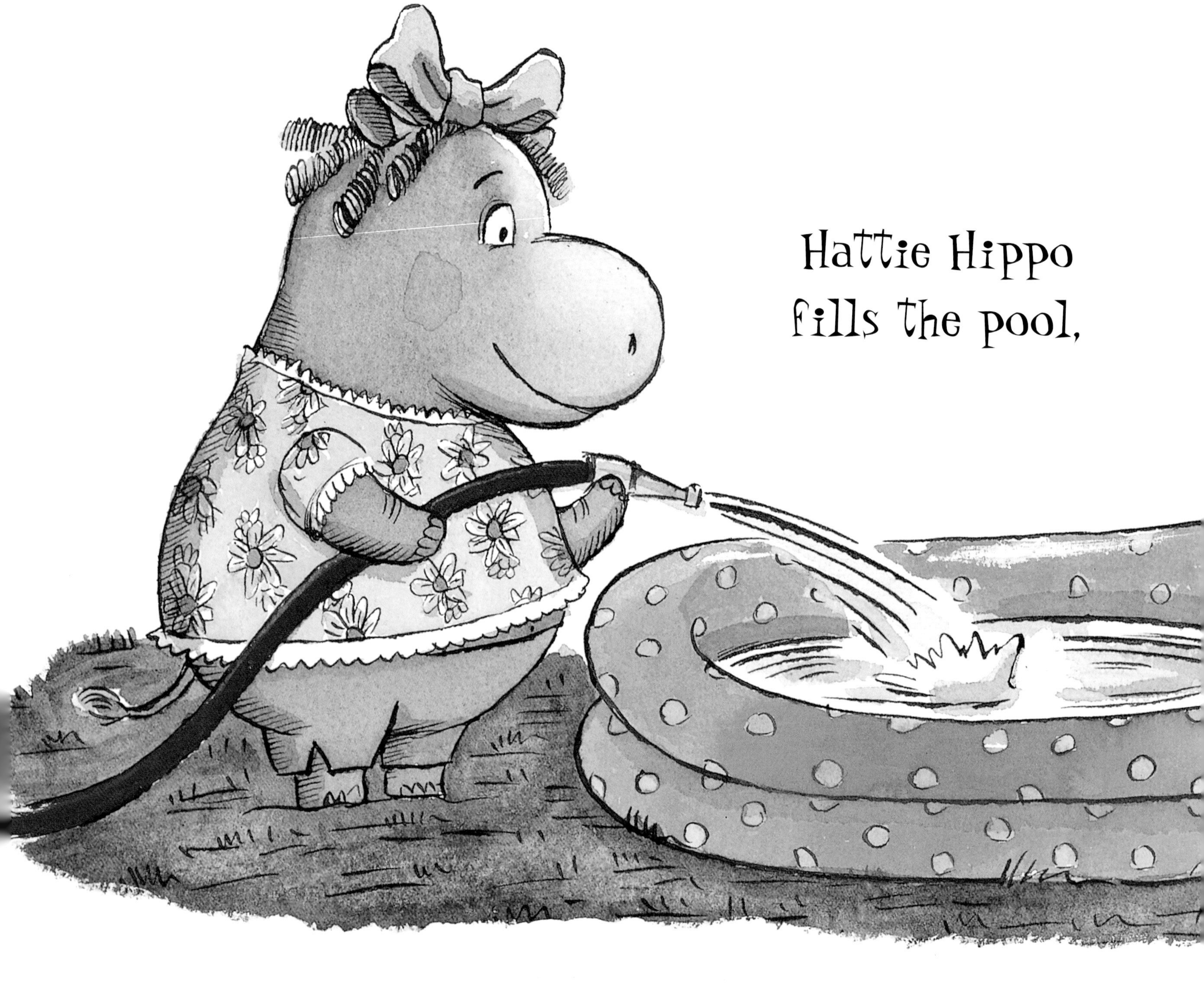

Hattie Hippo
fills the pool,

grabs a snorkel
and a mask.

Squeezing
into last year's suit
is an exhausting task!

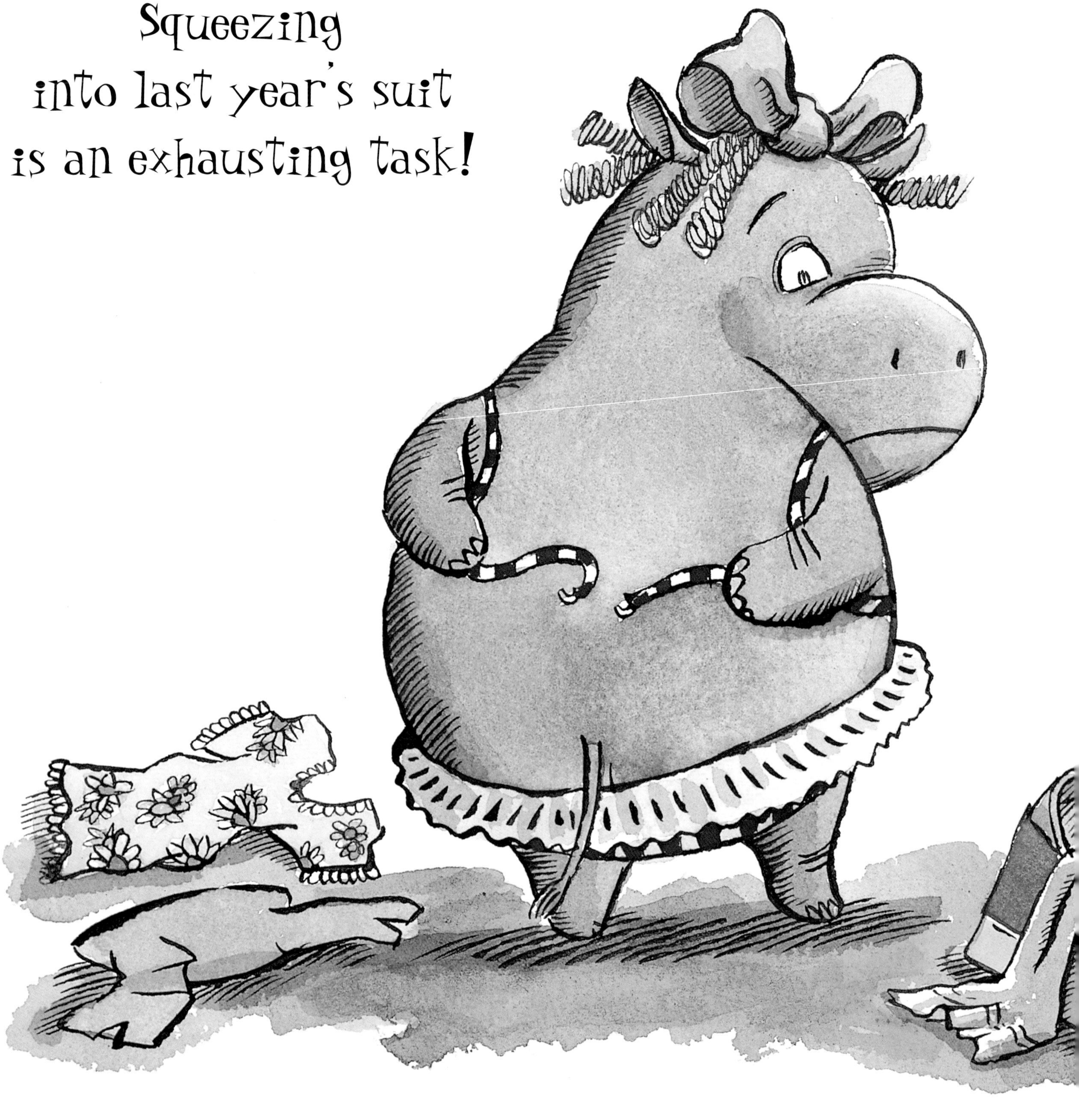

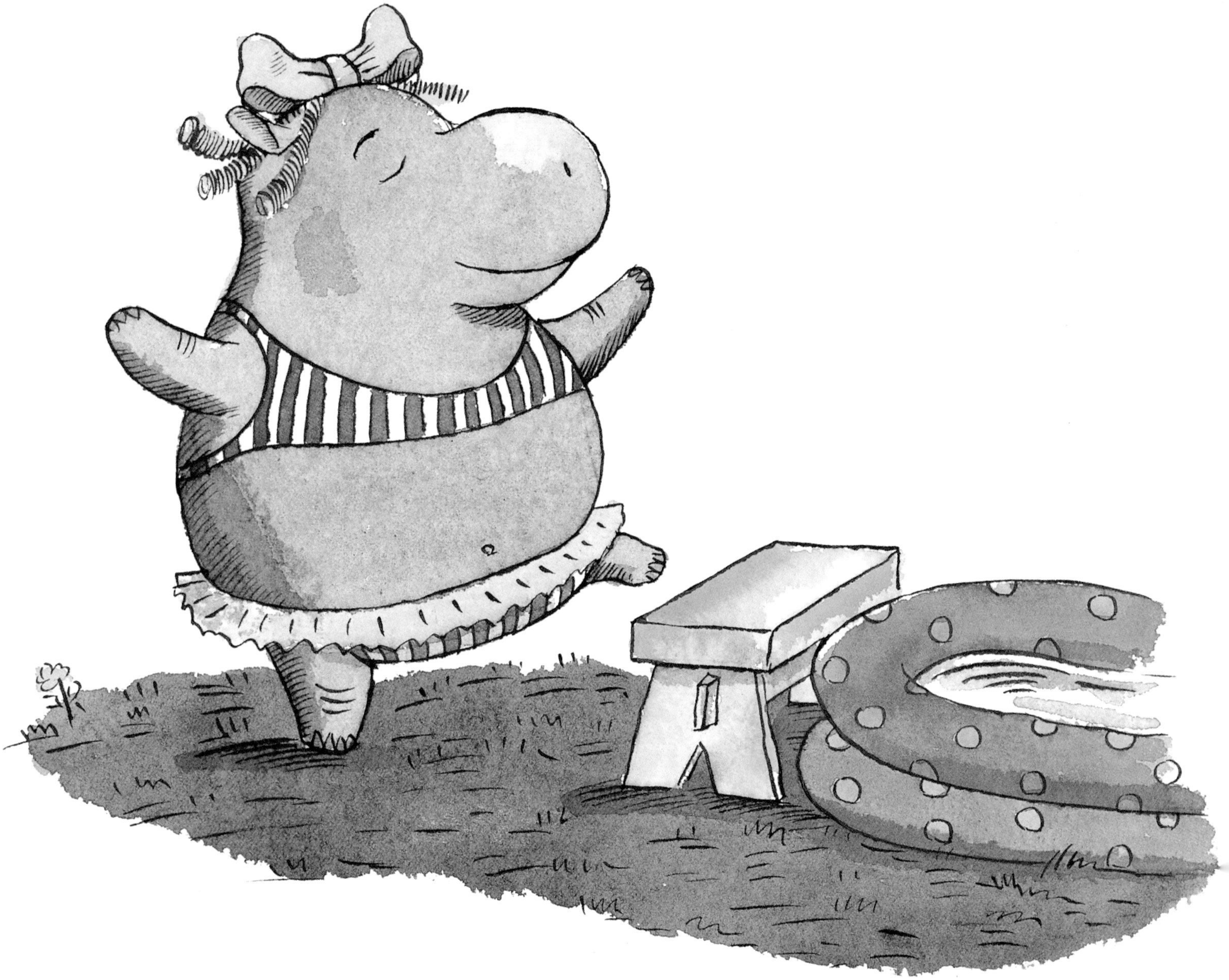

She takes a step
and holds her breath . . .

balances on one dainty toe,

then Hattie
boldly
cannonballs.

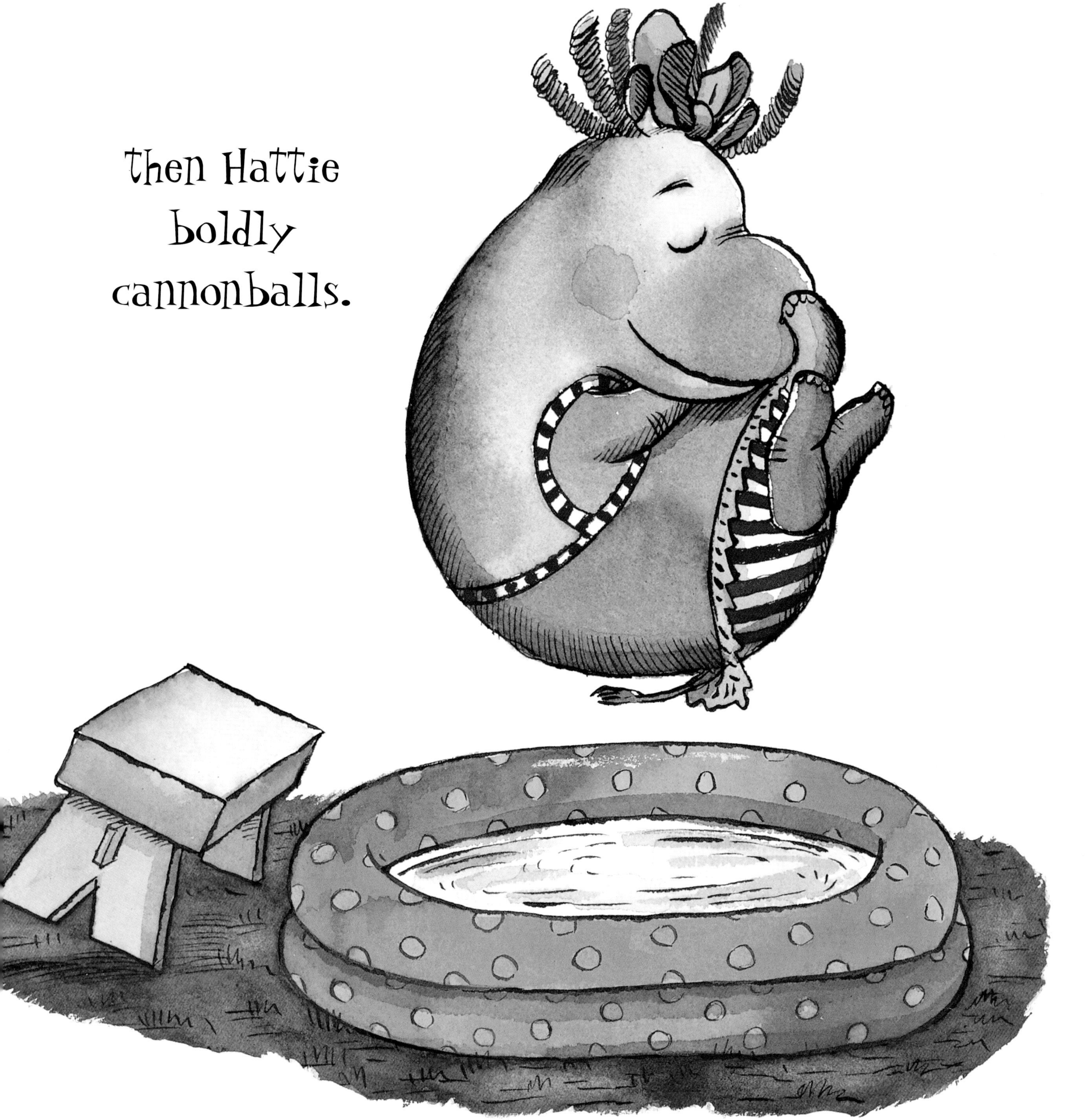

Oops!
Where did the water go?

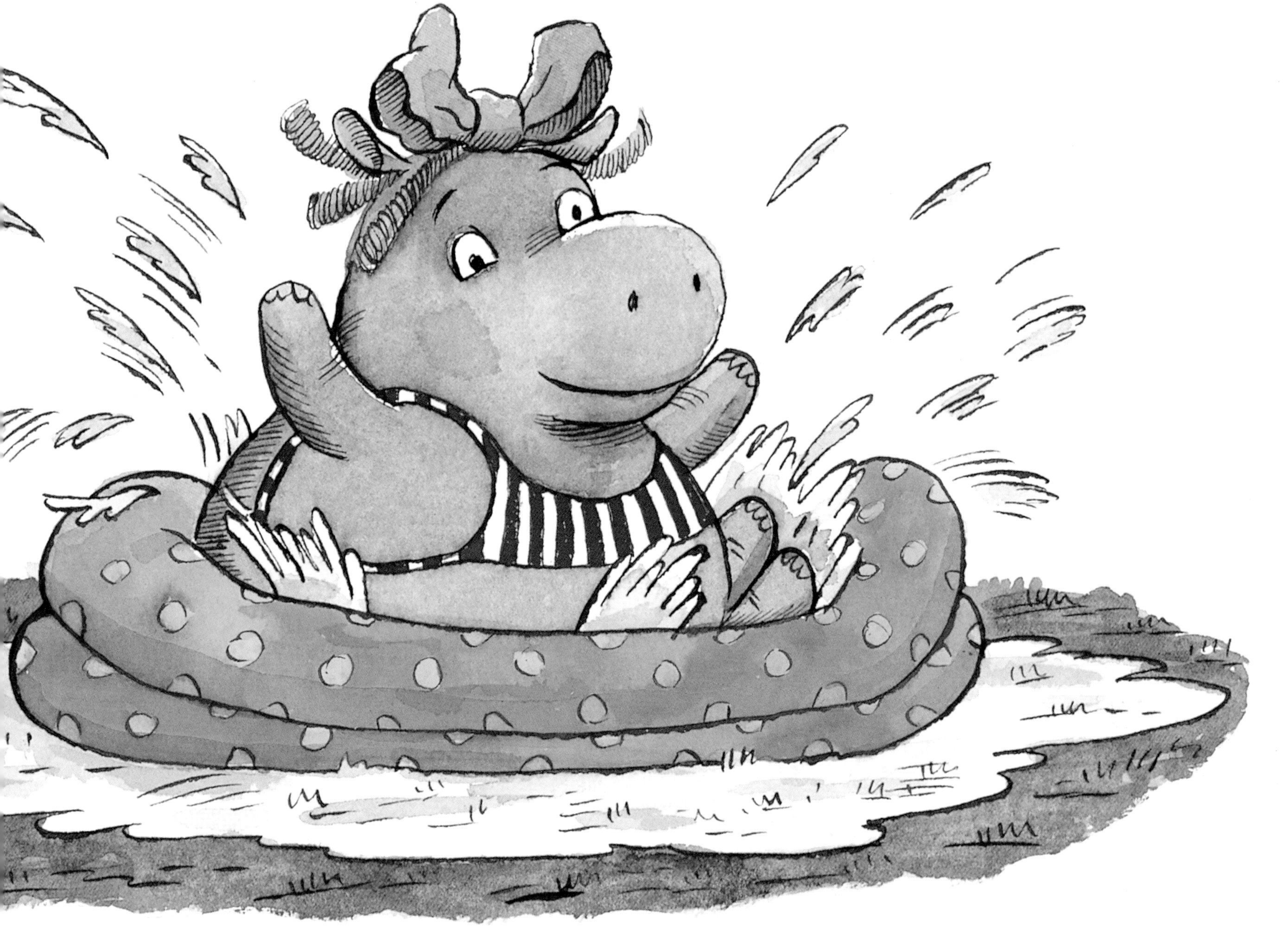

HIDE & SEEK

"Ready or not!"
Mama calls.

Where can Hattie be?
Behind the door?
Behind the stairs?

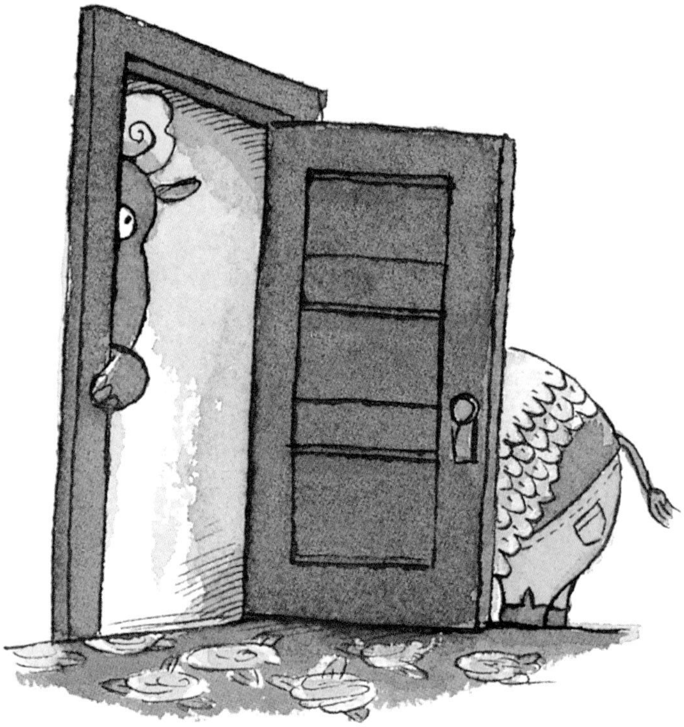

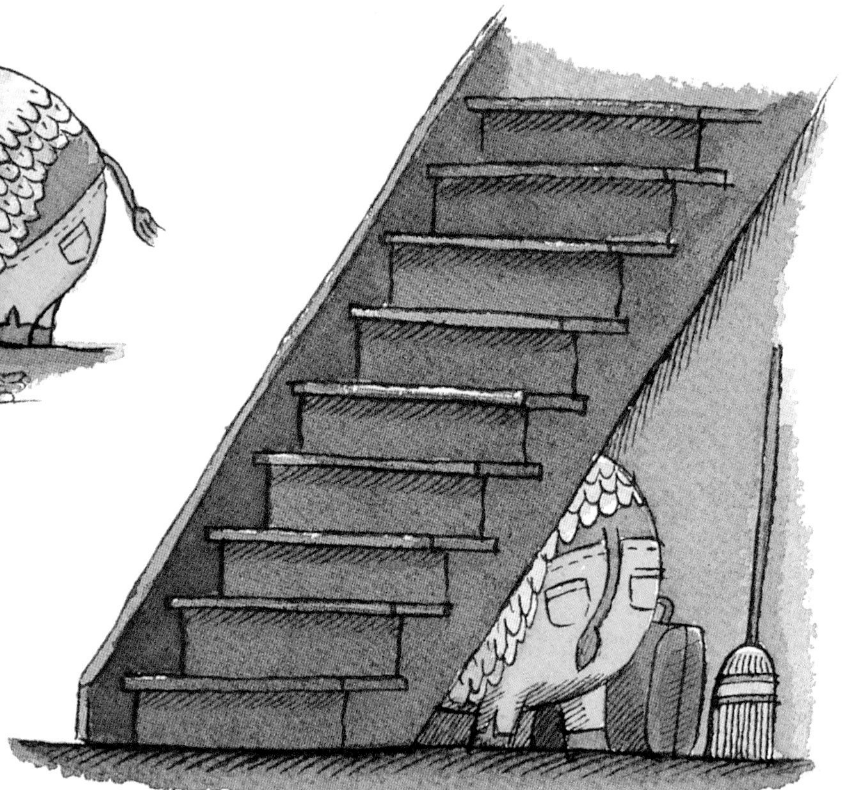

Beside the couch?

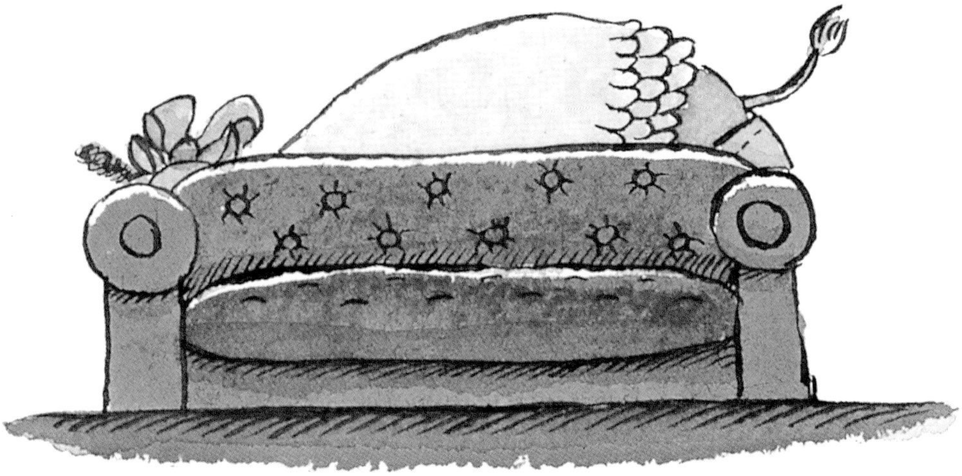

Up in a tree?

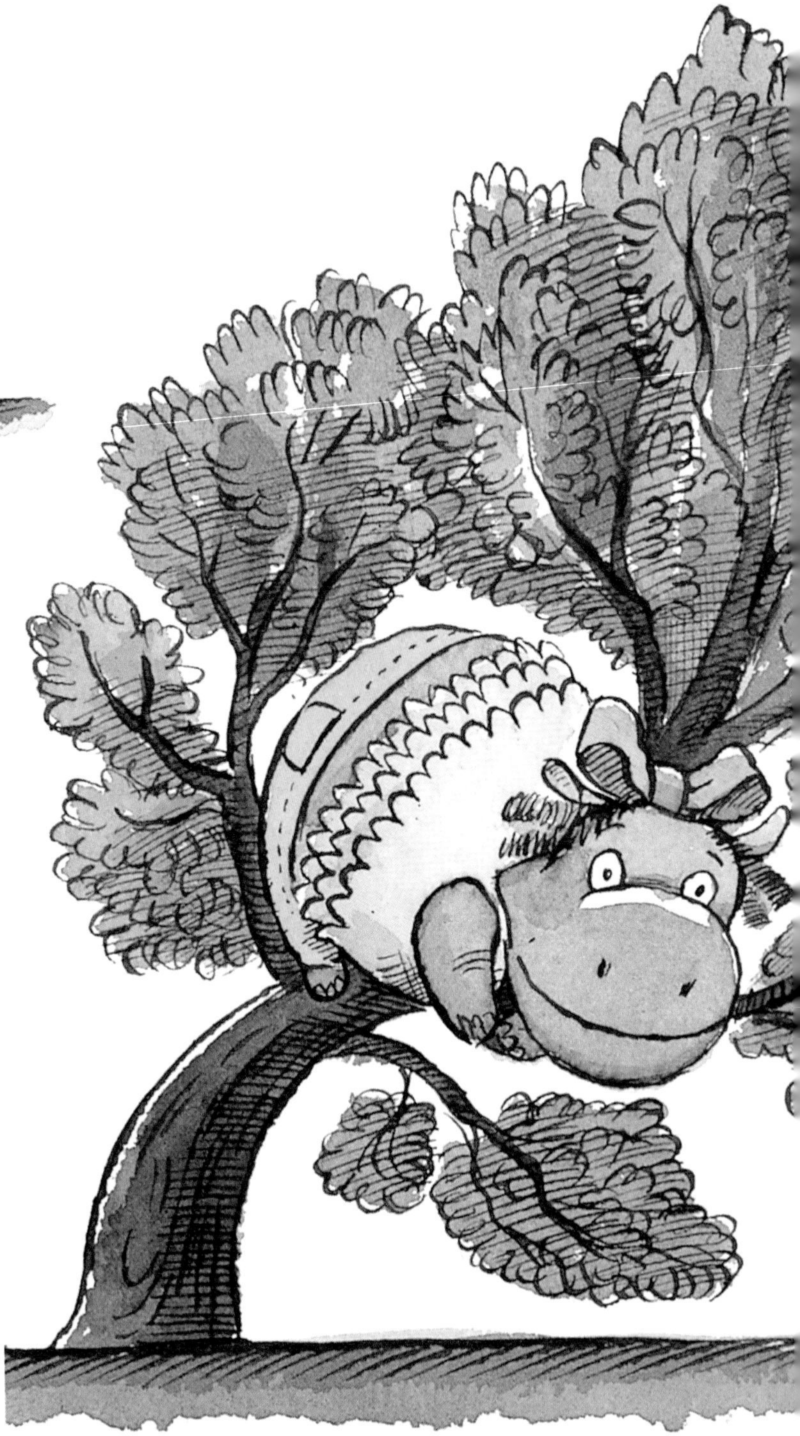

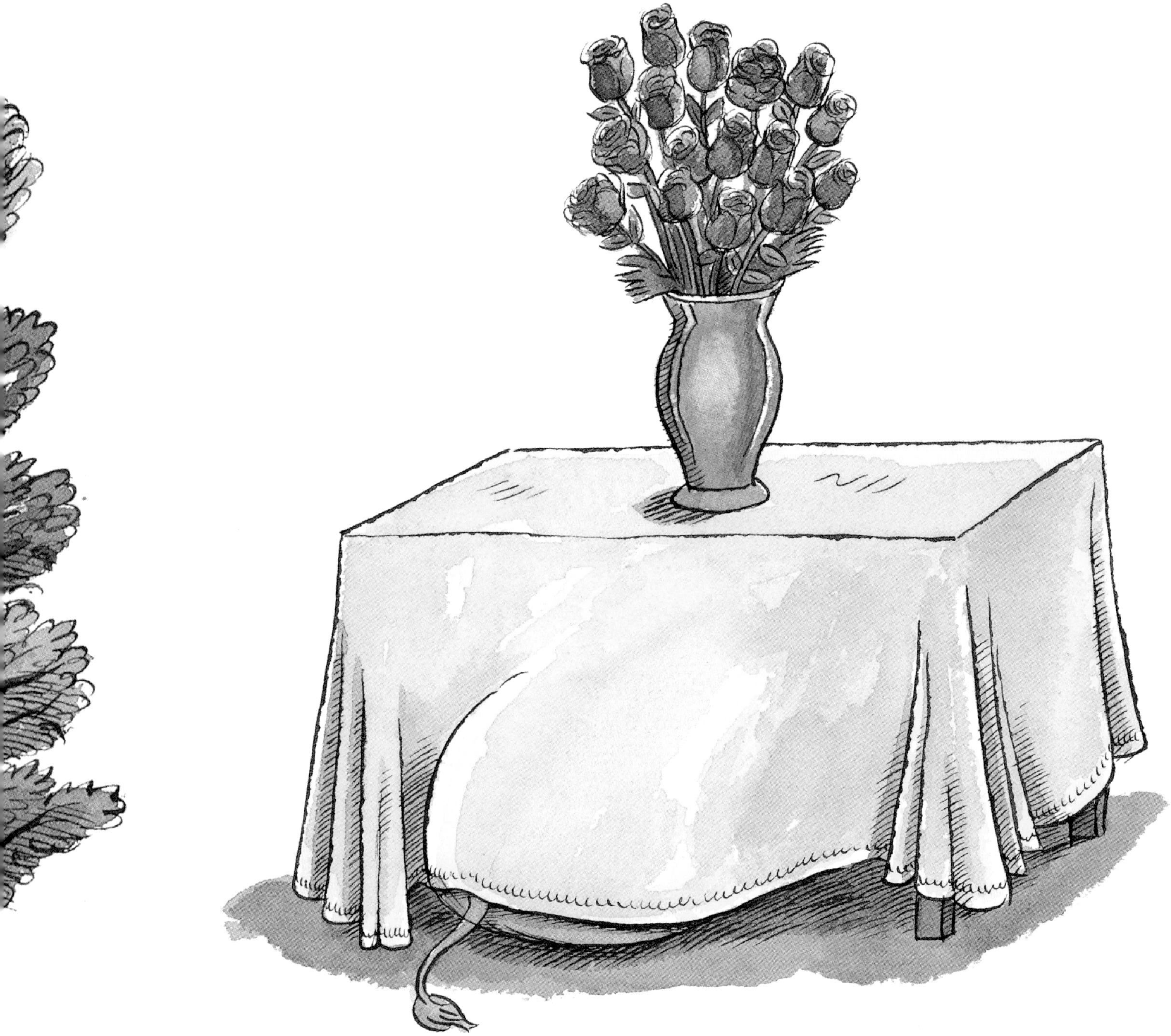

Hattie is good at hiding.
She doesn't make a peep.

"Aha!
I found you,"
Mama says.
But Hattie is fast asleep.